What's IN A POET?

Abhilekh Sharma

First Published in December 2022

ISBN: 978-93-5668-536-9

BLUEROSE PUBLISHERS

www.BlueRoseONE.com
info@bluerosepublishers.com
+91 8882 898 898

Cover Design:
Aman Sharma

Typographic Design:
Namrata Saini

Distributed by: BlueRose, Amazon, Flipkart

Dedicated to -

Every sleepless night that made me write all of it.

"If you can keep your head
When all about you
Are losing theirs and blaming it on you;
If you can trust yourself when all men doubt you
But make allowance for their doubting too."

–Rudyard Kipling

Author's Note

Poetry: Few words, thousand feelings. It has a world of its own; flawed yet wonderful, limited yet infinite. Indeed a world where we humans find the words which tell us how we really feel, in subtle but effective moments. Poetry stems from within the poet's soul and grows out as if it were an endless journey of bruises and beauty. There are a lot of times when you feel like your poem is going to reach the destination you want it to. And then there are other times, where you don't even feel like a poet. I know it's crazy but that's where the intelligence of a poet or a writer lies; in writing with all your heart. The prolific German-American poet Charles Bukowski rightly said, 'If you're going to try, go all the way. Otherwise, don't even start. There is no other feeling like that. It's the only good fight there is.'

I'm an emotional and sensitive person by nature and I believe that being emotional and sensitive were the catalysts in nurturing me as a poet. Having these attributes doesn't make one weak or utterly vulnerable, as many would like to believe. In fact, if we know how to direct our emotions and sensibilities, they become the very necessities which awake and sustain poetry in us. Now, to read a poem to get some momentary bliss is one thing but to actually understand the art of poetry, one needs to delve deep into the artistic intricacies of a poet because poetic appreciation is an art in itself. The most beautiful thing about poetry is that you can take a single word and write a whole world about it. Too fascinating to fathom, isn't it? Whether you're new or are an ardent lover of poems, hold on to it. Don't leave. You may not have a person to go to, but you will always have your poems. "We don't read and write poetry because it's cute. We read and write poetry because we are members of the human race. And the human race is filled with passion. And medicine, law, business, engineering, these are noble pursuits and necessary to sustain life. But poetry, beauty, romance, love, these are what we stay alive for." –John Keating (Dead Poets Society).

I welcome you to this journey of self-exploration, love, heartbreaks, healing and hope. Come, let's find out what's in a poet.

-Abhilekh Sharma

Contents

1. Inner child

Heal yourself
My inner child
It's time to finally grow
Your soul needs no more bruises
Hold on and let them go

You owe yourself
The greatest of loves
The sunrays beyond the clouds
Go find your peace in the silence of self
And not in the illusion of crowds

Do for yourself
Everything that you must
With no harm to another soul
Human life isn't a hamster wheel
Living is it's greatest goal

2. When nobody's watching you

Face that trigger
Fight that rage
Fix that mindset
Fly out of that cage

It's easy to look sane
When the crowd has eyes on you
But the real struggle lies
When nobody's watching you

You're stuck with yourself
In fear of defeat
Move away from that monster
Crush that voice with your feet

3. Greatness

Your success, your failure
Of the days gone by
Won't lead to the future
Unless you try
To rise beyond all
That you have gained and lost
Greatness is elusive
Only legends know it's cost

4. *You are my broken heart*

I came bearing my heart for you
And gave you all of it
You took, touched
Broke it down
And then turned my love into guilt
It's a terrible mess
The heaviness in my chest
Not a single word is left
In this dried up poet's empty hands
To give the ruin a rest

5. *How much do they pay for a broken heart?*

How much do they pay for a broken heart?
Coz I'm planning to sell mine right away
In this economy I can't care less
Just measure the pieces
And give me the cash
'But why would someone buy it?' you ask
'What could possibly be a broken heart's task?'
Then darling you're too new to know
The child in you is yet to grow
You see; the movies, the songs and dances
Are filled with many such broken pieces
From legendary heartbreaks
To silent goodbyes
From paintings of yore
To writings of the wise
The writer, the painter, the actor, the singer
The art and the artist, the story and its teller
All creativity comes from agonizing pain
Yet it beauty pours down like soothing rain

6. *Stone*

I have loved you in pieces
I have loved you as a whole
I gave you my all
And you turned me down cold
How long does it take?
For a stone to really feel
I have waited for a lifetime
I'll wait for another
Rather than heal

7. Smile

No, don't let my smile delude you
It's here just for it's goddamned sake
It's a lie I wear for survival
Coz who cares even if it's fake?
It's the same with all of them
The machines that we call people
They come and go
Like homeless winds
Bringing storms to leave us cripple
But that doesn't mean
You can resort to tears
This world won't shelter pain
In spite of all your heartbreaks
And your helpless screams
You can do nothing but
Pretend to be sane!

8. Brightest star

You're a blessing
Who curbed all my curses
In my sky
You're the brightest star
You hear me
In my silences too
You're the nearest
Even from afar

9. To love or not to love?

To love or not to love?
The flight of an innocent dove

To hold or to let go?
The sea has sadness in it's flow

To live or to die young?
The words of a half written song

10. Persistent heart

This heart has broken a hundred times
Yet how it lives and breathes!
Persistent, it keeps sailing through
A thousand turbulent seas!

11. Sea

You gave and gave
So much of yourself to them
Yet they made you feel so empty
It's they who lost
A forever with you
And yet here you are with anxiety

Don't let them take
Anymore of you
The river can't fathom the sea
Keep them safe
Your heart and your love
The right eyes will one day see

12. Light posts

I think this is what happens
When loneliness defeats your soul
You see people
And so many of them
That it's almost blinding
Their presence is fleeting
Like rays from light posts at night
And as you cross them all
While finding your way home
You wonder if
They could wipe out the darkness in you

13. Bridges

I wish I could burn all bridges
And come to you at once
If only life would've been fair
Love would have gotten a chance

So, let's meet in an alternate reality
Where no rules can bind hurts
If only there was a way out
You and I could have been us

14. *Unearthly*

Why is love so unearthly?
That, even everyday words are less
To make sense of how it feels like
Oh, this lover's a complete mess!

15. The wait

You are right next to me
Right here, on my mind
Your voice from last night
That sleepy laughter
Still echoes
I smile in peace
But there's something incomplete after that
Something beautiful though
The wait
To hear you talk again
Stubborn, this time doesn't go

16. I

I'll give rise to chaos
I'll burn myself in flames
I'll drink the enemy's blood
I'll die for true friends

I'll kill your gut for money
I'll fight to get you food
I'll bet on all that's evil
I'll live for all that's good

I'll wait for all of eternity
I'll snatch time out of your hand
I'll cry for all your miseries
I'll laugh at your helpless end

17. A human's world

Neither a man's world
Nor a woman's
We are all equal here
It's a human's world my friend
Barring all races and creeds
We ought to see throuhh only our deeds
Languages should make us send
All the love before we bring the end
No heart, no humanity
The world is paying its price
Not a trace of human dignity
Helpless, the future cries
What a world we had dreamt of
To live and grow with pride
What a world we are left with
Both rivers and hopes have dried
We beg and shout with anger
For the food that doesn't end hunger
We crawl and cry to exist
Under tyranny's cold blooded fist
The only truth left
Is that the end is painfully near
It's the mother earth's pain
That we all must fear
The earth thus has its way
To tell us of its wrath
Yet humans have no nerve

To speak a word of worth
Death and disease don't see
Of what religion a man might be
Knowledge and kindness will free
Every mind that's become an amputee
Women and men alike
Each human is a part of this fight
When reason will defeat the riot
Every child will see a better day's sight

18. Love

An euphoria of emotions
New and bright
Running through my core
Curing each crevice
They say its love
The most beautiful feeling
I say its life, an endless healing
Even a lifetime is less
To feel it, to express
For we don't live just life
But the love that it has
Or else what would we breathe for?
For what would we smile?
I'll be the road, you be my journey
Giving us a meaning every mile
Love is a dream, a battlefield
Where together, a home you both build
And slowly, your own heart grows
Helping dispel another heart's flaws

19. A writer's love

When a writer falls in love with you
You become an effortless muse
Of an endless story
Your eyes become poetry
Your touch, a touch of beauty
You are felt like
Raindrops in a desert
As your love mends
The writer's broken heart
And you live a different forever
Giving life to ink and paper

20. Dear Poet

Dear poet
Will you write me a poem?
With your fearless, mighty pen?
The one with which you vowed
To change the world as much as you can
From a world of crime
To one of creation
From a world of darkness
To one of determination
You are torn between relentless regrets
Its life, which is meant to be a mess
Yet between these roadblocks of fate
Your soul shall never lose faith
You're a fighter, fighting a restless mind
You are a giver of love and humankind

21. *You are a poem*

You are a poem
For poetry lives in your thoughts
If this world is a treasure
Its gold is your words

22. Newfound waves

Out of sight but never out of mind
You are the home
My heart will always find
You are the light my darkness craves
You are the ocean of my newfound wave

23. Can't talk like a lover

You know I can't talk like a lover
I try, my lips shiver
Don't know how others do it
But I try
You're a chance I can't quit
No fancy words to please you
No sweet nicknames too
But I'm the one with a soul to give
So much love, it'll be hard to weave
Words aren't tough
Until feelings catch them rough
Do you hear what I don't say?
Losing you is a fear
I can't convey
You're the breath I trust with my life
Your voice, my healer
My blood, your knife
Look into my eyes when words will fail to tell
How much I want you; my heaven, my hell
Let's not say much
And listen through our touch
Words may but love never hurts
As this silence bestows the beauty in us

24. Craving to love

I'm someone who craves to express
Not too much yet not too less
Your love gives air
For my words to breathe
And my soul dances
To its rhythm underneath
We are a dream
I don't want to wake up from
You're my desire
Wishful and warm
Deep down my heart
You have become an art
A poem, a love song
Beyond every right
And every wrong

25. He doesn't understand poetry

He doesn't understand poetry
Says words aren't really his thing
And I fail to fathom why
My words need only his feeling
He doesn't understand poetry
Says love is subtle otherwise
But I ask him what love is
Without words to pay it's price?
He doesn't understand poetry
Says eyes can talk much better
Yet I tell him how words can save
Two hearts that are sinking together

26. *When you love a man*

Give a man all that a woman must
But never let him
Take your love for lust

27. *Why to wait*

Don't bleed my heart
Once broken, it will always hurt
Go away silently
Don't wait for this smile to feel sorry
There's a way
For even a forever to get away
So why to wait
For love to become hate?

28. Just another heartbreak

It's just another day
Of feelings coming
And going away
You keep telling me
That yours will stay
No matter what comes our way
I say you don't have to
Even you can leave like others do
And I wouldn't even ask you why
I know how to live through pain
My life is nothing but a silent cry
How much can one break
A heart that's already broken?
Your truth was a beautiful lie
My peace, you have already taken

29. Cigarette

Pass me that cigarette, hey you
Let my lips taste
What yours tasted too
At least in my imagination
Your cold heart can make some exception
It won't be a kiss as such
I know you don't want one as much
As you would want to look me in the eye
And ask me that I loved you why
Yet again, like always, you won't
As distance from me is all you want
We couldn't have the love I had
Which was enough
For times both, good and bad
It's burning slowly in pain
My mind bearing all its strain
And as your memory gets older and older
I will know this even better and better
That what we had
Wasn't some love to beheld
It was a cigarette
Anyway meant to end

30. The echoes of yesterday

If only forgetting
Was as easy as forgiving
Life would have been easy
And the mind won't be crumbling
Into fragments of memories
Of long gone cravings
A need to erase
The scars of that phase
A scary mess
Every night, sleepless
A heavy heart has nothing to give
From a clouded head
Hurt can never leave
The echoes of yesterday
Haunting till this very day
Yet it is no reason to fall
Hold on, time has it's own call
For what's a human if not strong?
Life is all about
The right after the wrong

31. An impossible truth

You're a scar
A battle, a war
That I left fighting years ago
But the pain it gave
Would never go
You are my yesterday
Ruining my today
We were a painful lie
An illusion, retribution
My heart's reason to die

32. A part of me

A part of me
Is going away with you
Don't look back
As you leave my heart
My traces you won't find
From you, I have learned to hide
No looking at your eyes
And everything in between
We won't say goodbyes
No last words for comforting
Only our silence will know
All that would be left unsaid
And all that was said too
We'll pretend like we are alright
And heartbreaks will echo
As we leave each other behind

33. The lone wolf

Walking on and on
Against the tides of time
A journey written by the stars
From the eyes of humans it hides
Battling one's own destiny's path
It goes on with an endless wrath
From all around the world
Come those testing voices
To make or break life
Through a plethora of choices
Daunting days, full of despair
Many a swollen wounds to repair
Secrets to not tell ever
Not a soul to give a forever
Thus escaping the slaughters
By worldly butchering traps
The lone wolf goes to create
Its own path towards greatness

34. Leaders

Blended with the grace of
Unbent dignity
Leaders are the home to
Pride and integrity
A mind of motivation
A heart of true passion
Leaders show the path to
Selfless dedication
Truth is the one great virtue they own
Courage is what their journeys have shown
They know that for one to truly win
One must know to gracefully fail
For those are the ones
Whose names the world
Will hail alike in peace and war

35. Odd one out

Without the crowd
Strong and proud
Within the soul
Reaching the goal
Aloof from the judgments
One mind, no fragments
Away from the dirt
A beautiful heart

36. Stand your ground

Stand your ground
Even when your feet trembles
This world's a tricky place
Even the dumb here mumbles
They will test and test you more
Until you fall flat on the floor
Jealousy is the disease they spread
Don't lose your soul in this unworthy thread
Give yourself the growth you need
Leave their ego for them to feed
Nothing ever comes
At the cost of one's peace
If your ship is strong
The waves will cease

37. The Mighty Pen

I will train my pen
To defeat the swords
That would come its way
To defy my words
Ink which will write
Verses true and deep
Will flow from within
Its courageous nib
Justice will find life
Through the force of my pen
The future will be bright
In spite of today's rain

38. How Far?

How far would your heart reach?
After that forever you had will slip away
And you will find that
Expectations are nothing
But a trap for weak hearts

How far would your mind wander?
When it will realize
Over and over again that
Dreams are nothing
But a lie to reality

How far would your soul search?
For peace and for love
Even when it will know that
This world is nothing
But a web of comforting illusions

39. You will know

You will know
When things will start to tremble
When people will fade away
And again you will stumble
Mistakes will knock on your door again
You will open it thinking you're only human
You will know when you should let go
Yet you will not let yourself do so
Running and running
In the same circles with frustration
You will again and again
Bear fruitless exhaustion
But for once and only once being strong
If you would ask yourself
Where you went wrong
There won't be a soul who could let you down
And you will still know how to swim
Long after you drown

40. Strength

Chasing my dreams
Beneath their reality
Embracing my struggles
Against their apathy

41. Let it be

Let forgiveness always be there
Make strength reside within, don't fear
Let truth speak through your heart
No lie shall ever be thy guard
Let hope be the gateway
For life to find it's own way
Let belief be the guide
To light a darker night
Let love be the word
Bringing peace to this hateful world
Let art be the language
Spreading the beauty of knowledge
Let courage be the path
For the brave to face any wrath

42. The sun will shine

The sun will shine
Through the light of divine
Which no darkness can confine
And no doubt can define

43. I free myself

I free myself
From me and mine
Having all the doubts
Which shadow my shine
Neither future constraints
Nor bindings of the past
Can ever keep me from
Making my dreams last
I will trace through ways
Unseen, unfound
I will earn my treasure
And be proudly home bound
As long as I know
My truth, my meaning
No illusion can harm
My freedom, my beginning

44. Freedom

Who will tell the night to stay?
What will show the wind its way?
Freedom shall win the test of time
Its passion is only a sinless crime

45. The world through my eyes

A canvas of divinity
Nature is serenity
The world's a wonder
Eyes could only grow fonder
I have seen that love can
Take away any hatred
Unity isn't just
The blood in red
A word of sweetness
Heals even the heartless
When a smile can make a day
Why does heaven need another way?
Kindness is the way to live
In one and all, you shall believe
See the world as a beautiful possibility
Find the road to a euphoric infinity

46. Art of the heart

My heart is an art
That no hurt
Can tear apart
It's a survivor
A shield
It knows all pain
Deserves to be healed

47. I smile a lot, they say

I smile a lot, they say
But little do they know
How my survival finds its way
Pain is a part of life I know
In spite of it I dare to grow
What a world it would be?
Without a beautiful smile
Some strength to remember happiness
And to walk another mile
My heart will never lose itself
To the judgment of words
For one true smile is stronger
Than a thousand strong swords

48. The fire

You're a fire
Of boundless desire
You glow, you grow
Like a never ending flow
Your heart is made of light
There's no darkness you can't fight

49. Life

Life
A bed of thorns
And roses alike
Both beautiful and scary
Whether you like or dislike
It gives you hopes
Higher than the sky
And gives you wings
To fall and then fly
It's a poison, a nectar
A serious banter!
Laugh with it
Love, you shall receive
No heart shall be cold
Only give and forgive
With a will
A way comes out
So make life a belief
Never live in doubt

50. Bar

Beers and bongs
Cigarettes and shots
Numb is my mind
Blurry, its thoughts
Would a glass of wine
Make everything fine?
If not, maybe some whiskey
I'm sure one glass won't be risky
It's dark outside, a dark midnight
Yet inside here are darker souls
Under the brightest lights
If this is the shine
We have to chase
To get away from
That endless race
Then better I run
To a faraway place
Where tired hearts get true solace
With nights to sleep
And stars to keep
Sunrises to rise
And sunsets to cease

51. Time loop

Tick tock, tick tock
Time's flying, look at your clock
Fast pace, life's a race
Slow feet, life's a waste
Run, run for your life
Wait, wait you have to also thrive
From your beginning till your end
Time will roll you in it's long hand
You don't know the future
The present, you don't want
The past, you cannot change
Time sure knows how to haunt!

52. Year after year

Year after year
You promise yourself
To grow out of your
Own stuck up self
Year after year
You ask your dreams
How long will they take?
To hear your fading screams
Year after year
You lose people who were to stay
But your heart opens its door
Giving new people their way
Year after year
You watch your hopes break
Still you go on
Being beautiful and brave
Year after year
You feel like trying no more
Yet you survive every time
As that's what winners are for

53. Multiverse

What if there's really
An universe beyond?
Another reality
To live and behold
Where life is easy
And nature is taken care of
An unbelievable story
For a lifetime to live off

Hatred, pollution
Preposterous destruction
We are sadly made of
This hopeless collection

Away from the chaos
That we call earth
What if there's a world
Where humans actually find their worth?

54. The view from my college window

Standing amidst the crossroads
Of life, youth and ambitions
Burdened by the price of
Ageing parents' expectations
To grow up was to forget
The long lost childhood I had
Home is now a heart too far
Life ahead is a frightening blur
To be an adult is a curse they don't see
A freedom in which one’s not truly free

55. Adulting

Sleep deprived, half asleep
From the nine to five
Corporate clench
I'm racing against a clock
Which gives me nothing
But an endless wrench
You see, it's tiresome
This rat race
Is too gruesome
And since it gives my family
It's food and its roof
I can't really escape it
No risk is worth their good
I'm sitting here
On this worn out, old bench
Looking at what lies ahead
An incomplete, rough trench
Adulting
cannot be more daunting
I wish I were a child again
Dreams of those days
Were easier to sustain
Existential crisis at its best
I have forgotten
What it was like to rest

56. Letters to the sunset

When the sky paints itself
With hues of the sun
When the day falls for the night
Awaiting moonlight's return
My eyes write letters
Of unspoken words
A heart to heart
Of unmet roads

57. Silent beauty

There's a beauty in this silence
Which the setting sun can tell
There's music in this wind
Where my heartbeat's song shall dwell

58. Tired poet

Poets should never fall in love
Poetry enslaves them for that
You see, love is a distraction
And this heart, a stubborn beast
Wondering in places unknown
A vagabond of a mind
Worlds of words to give
Oceans of love to find
And some poetry takes form
From a tired poet's pen
An incomplete story
A lover's disdain

59. The lonely bird

The lonely bird
That sings alone
Its voice
That reaches nobody
Such a melancholy
This life becomes
When one always
Longing for somebody

60. Lovelorn

Love craves to fall right on your arms
And look deep into those eyes
It's a romantic's dream, my love
A heartless world's despise
But I'm a lovelorn
What worthwhile can I say?
For shadows
That don't hide together
The light eventually
Separates their way

61. Misplaced

When loneliness looms
And the heart feels weak
Not a thing seems worthy
For a fallen leaf to seek

It's a sad truth
To live with all
And yet with none

No home to stay
No escape to run

62. *Timing*

Neither get lost in the future
Nor dwell in the past
Be in this very moment
Let your peace of mind last
Time is a mysterious enemy
But a friend if mindfully used
This is your time to live
And leave no time misused

63. Prisoner of thoughts

Dwelling on my deluded mind
I'm clueless; where to start, where to wind
My thoughts are bars
Hiding my reason behind
My head is sick
The heart doesn't know what to seek
Life is stuck in a self-made feud
Reality is indeed very rude
'Doesn't it hurt?' I ask myself
'It doesn't heal.' I answer myself

64. Find me some words

Is the sky dark?
Or darker are my thoughts?
Who am I fighting this for?
With my own mind
Ripping me like swords?

65. God men

For the sake of religion and god
What not have these god men sought?
To corrupt the purpose of being
Or the hymns of hatred to sing?
If there is someone above the rest
Would he call this world a just place?
As humans kill in his name
Is worshipping simply a survival game?
Blame and shame others
You might gain something
As god has simply become
A mere human thing

66. *The deprived can only dream of*

I want to create a world
Where a human's right
Would not be a matter to fight

Where some food and a roof
Would not be something which
The deprived can only dream of

67. An Existence

A lifeless life
An effort to survive
To breathe at least
If not really thrive
I'm empty inside
My outside, crowded
Voices piercing
My ears beheaded
I can't win
I can't lose
I'm a stone
A painless bruise
As hated as grime
I'm worth no dime
As dreary as time
To chaos I climb

68. Songbirds

The sun is shining big and bright
Life is yet a looming night
Grass is greener on the other side
Yet this side suffers countless plights
Trees shed leaves, new ones grow
Yet stillness is what all cripple minds know
Winds hide words of a heartfelt song
For which those forgotten songbirds long
Somewhere a voice in melancholy cries
And again an unheard melody dies

69. *Watch Out*

Watch out
The imposters are hiding
Somewhere behind
All that shinning
Save yourself
Here you forever shouldn't dwell
For this world is nothing
But a man eating cannibal

70. Mind of a devil

A long, narrow boulevard
It gets scary as you walk
Darker than the night sky
Here evil escapades lurk
A trap of a sinful memory
Yet to innocence it belongs
Suffocating since a lifetime
For freedom it thus longs
A destroyed mind
That has no clue
What to do
What not to do
Don't go near
Till death you'll fear
Don't go away
It wants you near

71. Apocalypse

One world, infinite people
Came the myth of good and evil
One tells a lie, another numbs a truth
Hatred reigns all,
No love to bear fruit
This world is meant to end
No messiah to save it
No helping hand
A creation so divine since its inception
Should an apocalypse be its ultimate destruction?

72. Nerves

I feel everything
And then nothing
A whole another world
Inside my nerves, it's running
It stops every time I struggle
Emotions aren't a thing to haggle
To fight away those vibes
Of endless lows and highs
Life is indeed the hardest
It hears no sounds of cries
As pain comes only to the wounded
And peace only to the wise
So, if you really have the nerve
Then live like you feel nothing
Or die a slow death
With a hollow heart that keeps bleeding

73. My world at midnight

Beside my pillow
Deep at midnight
I keep away my sorrows
To rest aside
Then I close my eyes
To give them a world
Stars are so bright
It's a peaceful night.

74. Don't wake me up from my dream

Don't wake me up from my dream
Seeing reality, my mind will only scream
While running away from
The voices that drag me down
To destroy, break and wipe out
Whatever it is that I'm holding hard
Hopes, memories, magic and stories
Making me forget all my worries
If not in real but in illusion at least
As life is nothing but a heist of peace
And even if I sleep for this dream
Again and again
Don't wake me up
Reality has nothing for me to gain

75. Bottled up feelings

Up and up my blood rises
To storm out the pain
Of unfulfilled wishes

Some days it feels like
Everything's falling in place
Others seem
As if everything's a waste
All these efforts
Are they even worth it?
Or things would just end up
In an unknown dead pit
It's so hard to not think at all
Of how scary it would be
To rise once and then forever fall
What's blocking the way?
Why these anxieties wouldn't go away?
If everything's a question
How would one even find a solution?
You know sometimes it's not possible
We humans are impossible
No, no, don't hate me
I'm trapped, it's uneasy to be not free
Is love always so easy to get lost?
And make expressing emotions feel like worst?
What will it take for feelings to be heard?
Who would remember the words of this heart?

Will regrets get chances?
To heal without sadness
If you too share my voiceless wrath
You're simply another war not fought
If every day makes you feel like having an escape
Where would you run after losing every way you ever had?

76. We are fading

We are fading by the day
Nights seem too long to stay
No lights are shinning bright
Darkness is causing fright
We always find a way
At least that's what people say
But no one knows the truth
Or one ever should?
We don't know what we need
Broken relations often bleed
Everything, we think we have
But really it's only in our head
We are all stuck in the past
And the future's imposing way too fast
Nobody's dares to live in the present
Each moment's an unspoken torment

77. Shriveled

The dry leaves of autumn
Cover my sight
Some unknown fear
What shall I even fight?
This dreary, dreadful night
And the sound of a lost voice
Do I wish it to come back?
I can't even make that choice
Their constantly suspicious eyes
Lingering on my silence
What else can a shriveled soul do?
But wear the mask of reluctance
Suffocating inside a guilt
Escaping nothing and everything
Shivering like someone sinned
Everyday my limbs get killed

78. The light shall find the light

You are so much more
Than what you think you are
Look within
Your heart isn't far
Hold it with strength
And see what it's made of
Look within
Don't let your soul get lost
There's a reason behind you
Your very existence
Don't claim it worthless
In the illusion of the everyday
Understand your own philosophy
It's the voice of your essence
The root of all your thoughts
Never underestimate your mind
Direct it towards greater consciousness
Through patience gaining of
Age old knowledge
That has surpassed all tests of time
Question everything
And go beyond
The grip of your mere surroundings
If you really want
To make sense of the world
Trust in your own self
For nothing else is

More certain and true
Than what constitute you
But don't imbibe ignorance
It's the enemy of one's growth
And if you search for the light
In the perpetual darkness of this world
Your purpose of being a human
The gift of your intelligence
Will find it's true calling
Because it's not what we achieve at the end
But the quest towards it
That matters in the truest sense

79. Half lit hearts

In long nights
A dreamer that never sleeps
Hidden from the crowd
A quiet girl screams
Roaming with heartbreak
The romantics of art
An old rose in her diary
Some lipstick stain on his shirt
Eyes that see rainbows
In skies that hide storms
A seeker of peace suffers
Symphony of endless wrongs
Days and days go by
On nights one can't even try
Life skips a beat
In these maze of unseen paths
Words fail to meet
A cacophony of half lit hearts

80. A falling flight

They say to fly higher
Is a true human desire
As to fall deeper
No soul could ask for ever
Alike million others like me
My soul too was a souring entity
I flew and flew and flew and flew
My wings were thus my only rescue
Until I fell
Deeper into the hell
Of unjust tides
Where only self-doubt flies well

81. Sunsets and memories

The sun sets away with all your memories
And the night wraps me again
With our incomplete stories

82. Dead inside

Silence, deep silence
And the ceiling fan hangs still
It's calling me to kill
Oh, these thoughts
My head, they ruin
I fight and fall
And crawl and crawl
Hands numb
Heart's cold
Silence, deep silence
As they don't like my voice
For it might hush their noise
Oh, these people
I sob, they see
Is it just them?
Or is life actually better with apathy?
I say and shut
From gut to rut
My eyes wide open
No hold of what might happen

83. My death

If somehow I die tomorrow
Don't shed tears on my grave
My existence was a myth
And my death wouldn't either be great
Don't stare at my lifeless body
It was lifeless even with breath

Don't pray
Souls don't rest in peace
It's a lie they tell
For their guilt to cease

This world has killed me enough
To die that one last death
With no more words to swallow
With no more fear to sweat

84. End

What if I end it all?
Bearing no more pain
To rise and fall
No more longings for
Love unrequited
No more wailings
By voices unwanted
Alone I lie
In the midst of this loneliness
Death is a sigh
Peaceful than those wishes
That died unfulfilled
Oh, my heart never healed!
Send me away
I don't belong to this world
How much more
Can a dead heart hold?
Will you remember?
My voice when I go away
Or will it also be?
Another forgotten runaway
Feed me some peace
My soul here is dying hungry
The light has begun to cease
Tragedy, tragedy!

85. After the end

After the end
When darkness will come
When silence will speak
When the pain will be numb
I will wake up
In a world other than this
And let my heart dare
To dream and live

86. Trying

I'm not weak
I'm trying to be strong
Tell me what's right
Only if you didn't do any wrong

87. Head bang

A head that bleeds
The regrets of deeds
All of its memories
The keepers of untold stories
It's a play of words
It's a war of thoughts
A victim of the mind
Heartless, unkind
If only I could break it
To a thousand pieces and quit
And not think another thought again
Having nothing to lose
Not a memory to regain

88. Hope

A roaring heart
A pale face
The unseen ways
Too tired to trace
Even cold feet
Comes at a cost
Unnerved once
Forever lost
Peace of mind
A mystery to find
The soul gets cold
This darkness is bold
Yet somehow
Hope fights defeat
So someday
Fear might retreat

89. Remains of an old diary

Lost pieces
Of all that is left
Deep inside me
They quietly rest
Cold, intense words
Filled with angst and desire
I often drink to them
The heart burns like a fire
You, peaceful memory
When did you leave?
It still feels unreal
I helplessly grieve
Torn, yellow pages
Of days gone by
Stories that hide
A weeping heart's cry

90. She's wounded like a warrior

She's wounded like a warrior
Like a coward she doesn't hide
Throw at her all the stones you want
In spite of them she will fight
A bleeding state of anarchy
Is her home that gently cries
Longing for days of freedom
Her faith in righteousness dies
This unending patriarchy
A reign of failed men
They say all men are equal
So why make place for a woman?
Every hour is a test of time
Even a voice becomes a crime
These battles will go on and on
Until her war is fought and won
The future will sure witness
A greater day for her pride
As she speaks up for her trueborn right
A world of womanhood will rise

91. *Persistence*

Find your calling before it's too late
Remember, love is the reason
To live out hatred
Take away all your dreams with you
They will be safe in someplace new
No eyes with suspicion
No mouths to speak ill
No minds with misguidance
No life against your will
Learn and learn
For the future to be great
Only wisdom is the weapon
To defeat a world of threat
Throw away all pain of the past
For peace is what wins at last
Good things take time
The patient one knows
Success is a river
With persistence it flows

92. You're my peace of mind

You're my peace of mind
You're my chaos too
So I keep telling my reckless heart
How I find love in you
You are a mystery
Your eyes are quiet
I long to unfold the story
Which beneath those eyes you hide

93. Ragamuffin

Wearing my scars
As badges of victory
Surviving my days
With a belief that's a mystery
Singing with the birds
Their homecoming rhapsody
Walking through life
A wonderful tragedy

94. *Let's have a drink tonight*

It's a lonely night
Let's have a drink
I don't think
I have any strength to over think
Sit, let's share some cheers tonight
To forget despair for a moment's delight
You can tell me those stories untold
And I'll listen with all my soul
Until I found that the night knew your way

95. I feel my pain

I feel my pain
They don't, they don't
Oh, what a pity these people
They float, they gloat
Out of gritty holes
Of dirt and decadence
A clever death sentence
To die while living
Dead since the beginning
Anarchy, apathy
A worldly strategy
To teach ignorance
To push the downtrodden
To die swollen deaths
On the dark road of vengeance

96. Sometimes

Sometimes there aren't any words
To express some exhausting thoughts
No reason to justify their endurance
No music to calm the loss

9 789356 685369

Printed by Libri Plureos GmbH in Hamburg, Germany